CORDUROY

CORDUROY

Story and Pictures by Don Freeman

PUFFIN BOOKS

To Sally Elizabeth Kildow
and Patrick Steven Duff Kildow,
who know how a bear feels about buttons

A bear's share of the royalties to the Freeman Family Trust from the sale of *Corduroy* goes to the *Don and Lydia Freeman Research Fund* to support psychological research concerning children afflicted with cancer.

PUFFIN BOOKS
Published by the Penguin Group
Penguin Putnam Books for Young Readers,
345 Hudson Street, New York, New York 10014, U.S.A.
Penguin Books Ltd, 27 Wrights Lane, London W8 5TZ, England
Penguin Books Australia Ltd, Ringwood, Victoria, Australia
Penguin Books Canada Ltd, 10 Alcorn Avenue, Toronto, Ontario, Canada M4V 3B2
Penguin Books (N.Z.) Ltd, 182-190 Wairau Road, Auckland 10, New Zealand
Penguin Books Ltd, Registered Offices: Harmondsworth, Middlesex, England

First published by The Viking Press 1968
Viking Seafarer Edition published 1970
Reprinted 1972 (twice), 1974, 1975
Published in Puffin Books 1976
3 5 7 9 10 8 6 4
Copyright © Don Freeman, 1968
All rights reserved

ISBN 0 14 050.173 8
Special Markets ISBN 978-0-14-241735-5
Not for resale
Library of Congress catalog card number: 77-71209

Manufactured in China

This Imagination Library edition is published by Penguin Group (USA), a Pearson company, exclusively for Dolly Parton's Imagination Library, a not-for-profit program designed to inspire a love of reading and learning, sponsored in part by The Dollywood Foundation. Penguin's trade editions of this work are available wherever books are sold.

Corduroy is a bear who once lived in the toy department of a big store. Day after day he waited with all the other animals and dolls for somebody to come along and take him home.

The store was always filled with shoppers buying all sorts of things,
but no one ever seemed to want a small bear in green overalls.

Then one morning a little girl stopped and looked straight into Corduroy's bright eyes.

"Oh, Mommy!" she said. "Look! There's the very bear I've always wanted."

"Not today, dear." Her mother sighed. "I've spent too much already. Besides, he doesn't look new. He's lost the button to one of his shoulder straps."

Corduroy watched them sadly as they walked away.

"I didn't know I'd lost a button," he said to himself. "Tonight I'll go and see if I can find it."

Late that evening, when all the shoppers had gone and the doors were shut and locked, Corduroy climbed carefully down from his shelf and began searching everywhere on the floor for his lost button.

Suddenly he felt the floor moving under him! Quite by accident he had stepped onto an escalator—and up he went!

"Could this be a mountain?" he wondered. "I think I've always wanted to climb a mountain."

He stepped off the escalator as it reached the next floor, and there, before his eyes, was a most amazing sight—

tables and chairs and lamps and sofas, and rows and rows of beds.
"This must be a palace!" Corduroy gasped. "I guess I've always
wanted to live in a palace."

He wandered around admiring the furniture.
"This must be a bed," he said. "I've always wanted to sleep in a
bed." And up he crawled onto a large, thick mattress.

All at once he saw something small and round.
"Why, here's my button!" he cried. And he tried to pick it up. But, like all the other buttons on the mattress, it was tied down tight.

He yanked and pulled with both paws until POP! Off came the button—and off the mattress Corduroy toppled, *bang* into a tall floor lamp. Over it fell with a crash!

Corduroy didn't know it, but there was someone else awake in the store. The night watchman was going his rounds on the floor above. When he heard the crash he came dashing down the escalator.

"Now who in the world did that!" he exclaimed. "Somebody must be hiding around here!"

He flashed his light under and over sofas and beds until he came to the biggest bed of all. And there he saw two fuzzy brown ears sticking up from under the cover.

"Hello!" he said. "How did *you* get upstairs?"

The watchman tucked Corduroy under his arm and carried him down the escalator

and set him on the shelf in the toy department with the other
animals and dolls.

Corduroy was just waking up when the first customers came into the store in the morning. And there, looking at him with a wide, warm smile, was the same little girl he'd seen only the day before.

"I'm Lisa," she said, "and you're going to be my very own bear. Last night I counted what I've saved in my piggy bank and my mother said I could bring you home."

"Shall I put him in a box for you?" the saleslady asked.

"Oh, no thank you," Lisa answered. And she carried Corduroy home in her arms.

She ran all the way up four flights of stairs, into her family's apartment, and straight to her own room.

Corduroy blinked. There was a chair and a chest of drawers, and alongside a girl-size bed stood a little bed just the right size for him. The room was small, nothing like that enormous palace in the department store.

"This must be home," he said. "I *know* I've always wanted a home!"

Lisa sat down with Corduroy on her lap and began to sew a button on his overalls.

"I like you the way you are," she said, "but you'll be more comfortable with your shoulder strap fastened."

"You must be a friend," said Corduroy. "I've always wanted a friend."

"Me too!" said Lisa, and gave him a big hug.